Princess Truly
I Am a Good Friend!

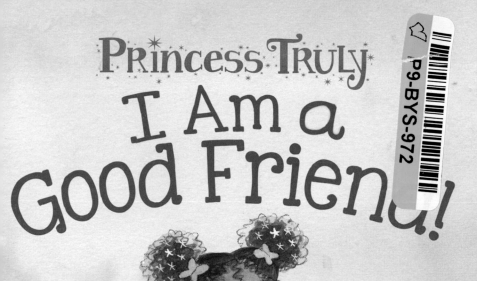

WRITTEN BY
Kelly Greenawalt

ART BY
Amariah Rauscher

**ACORN**™
SCHOLASTIC INC.

To my marvelous mom, Sherry, who tells the best
bedtime stories. — KG

For Rosie. — AR

Text copyright © 2021 by Kelly Greenawalt
Illustrations copyright © 2021 by Amariah Rauscher

Library of Congress Cataloging-in-Publication Data
Names: Greenawalt, Kelly, author. | Rauscher, Amariah, illustrator. | Greenawalt, Kelly. Princess Truly ; 4.
Title: I am a good friend! / by Kelly Greenawalt ; illustrated by Amariah Rauscher.
Description: First edition. | New York : Acorn/Scholastic Inc., 2021. | Series: Princess Truly ; 4 |
Summary: In rhyming text, Princess Truly strives to use her magic powers to be a good friend whether
it is in the park with her pug Noodles (who needs a little help making new friends), in the rainbow
clubhouse that she and her best friend are building, or at her very first sleepover.
Identifiers: LCCN 2020001310 (print) | ISBN 9781338676792 (paperback) | ISBN 9781338676808
(library binding) |
Subjects: LCSH: Princesses—Juvenile fiction. | Best friends—Juvenile fiction. | Friendship—Juvenile
fiction. | Stories in rhyme. | CYAC: Stories in rhyme. | Princesses—Fiction. | Friendship—Fiction. | African
Americans—Fiction. | LCGFT: Stories in rhyme.
Classification: LCC PZ8.3.G7495 Iad 2021 (print) | DDC [E]—dc23
LC record available at https://lccn.loc.gov/2020001310
LC ebook record available at https://lccn.loc.gov/2020001311

10 9 8 7 6 5 4 3 2 1   21 22 23 24 25

Printed in China   62

First edition, August 2021

Edited by Rachel Matson
Book design by Sarah Dvojack

New Friends

I am Princess Truly.
My best friend is my pup.

It is time to go play.

I need to wake him up.

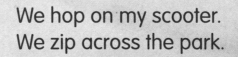

We hop on my scooter.
We zip across the park.

There is someone new here!
Sir Noodles starts to bark.

It's a girl and her pet!
The yellow parrot sings.

She lands in Noodles's spot
and flaps her fancy wings.

Noodles does not like this.
What is she doing there?

That spot belongs to **him**.
He does not want to share.

I say, "Nice to meet you."
She says, "My name is May."

Her bird is named Lemon.
I ask them both to play.

We try to play soccer,
but Noodles takes the ball.

When Lemon wants a treat,
Sir Noodles eats them all.

Noodles is not happy.
I give him a big hug.

It's fun to make new friends!
Do not be grumpy, pug.

When you are a good friend,
you take turns and you share.

When someone feels upset,
you listen and you care.

Our Rainbow Clubhouse

This is my friend Lizzie.
This is our new friend May.

All of our pets are here.
We want a place to play!

We will build a clubhouse.
We have so much to do.

Good friends work together.
They help each other, too.

We climb up the ladder.
Sir Noodles starts to shake.

Waffles tries to help him.
Paint crashes by mistake!

Lizzie tries to mop it.
She slips and spins around.

May tries to help her up,
and falls down on the ground.

My magic hair shines bright.
I need to save the day.

I zap up all the paint,
and now it's time to play!

It's a rainbow clubhouse.
The door is open wide.

I hang a welcome sign.
More new friends come inside.

Rocked to Sleep

It's our first sleepover!
We have fun things to do.

My friends are coming here.
Their pets are coming, too!

First, we watch a movie.

Next, we wear fancy clothes.

We eat purple cupcakes.

And then we paint our toes.

We put on our PJs.
The moon is high and bright.

We read some funny books.
Then we turn out the light.

Waffles is not tired.
He does not want to sleep.

With a little magic,
I'll teach him to count sheep.

hee
hee
hee

101 CAT JOKES

PUGTALES

He still is not sleepy.
There's one thing left to try.

I'll rock Waffles to sleep,
and sing a lullaby.

He is almost asleep!
Let's sing another song.

Best friends help each other.
All our pets sing along.

It's time to tuck him in.

Lizzie gives him a hug.

I get into my bed,
and snuggle with my pug.

About the Creators

Kelly Greenawalt is the mother of six amazing kids. She lives in Texas with her family. Princess Truly was inspired by her oldest daughters, Calista and Kaia. Some of Kelly's best buddies are animals. Especially the cows that live next door!

Amariah Rauscher spends most of her day drawing and painting, but she always makes time for her two furry dog friends, Nika and Felix. She gives them lots of treats, takes them for long walks, and never forgets to scratch them behind the ears.

Read these picture books featuring Princess Truly!

YOU CAN DRAW LIZZIE!

1 Draw the outline of Lizzie's face. Add her eyes.

2 Draw her nose, ears, mouth, and neck. Add her bangs.

3 Draw Lizzie's glasses.

4 Finish drawing her hair. Stack four circles coming down from both sides of her head to make the braids.

5 Add bows to her hair. Draw her shirt.

6 Color in your drawing!

WHAT'S YOUR STORY?

Princess Truly builds a clubhouse.
What would **your** clubhouse look like?
Who would help you build it?
How would you work together?
Write and draw your story!

scholastic.com/acorn